First published in Belgium and Holland by Clavis Uitgeverij, Hasselt – Amsterdam, 2016
Copyright © 2016, Clavis Uitgeverij

Copyright © 2017 for the English language edition: Clavis Publishing Inc. New York

Visit us on the web at www.clavisbooks.com

*My Good Morning* written by Kim Crockett Corson and illustrated by Jelena Brezovec

ISBN 978-1-60537-342-3

This book was printed in August 2017 at Publikum d.o.o., Slavka Rodica 6, Belgrade, Serbia

First Edition
10 9 8 7 6 5 4 3 2

# My Good Morning!

Clavis
**NEW YORK**

Kim Crockett Corson
& Jelena Brezovec

I wake up nice and early.
I had a *good sleep*.
Mommy and Daddy did not hear a peep.
It's a new day and **I'm ready to go**!
But Mommy and Daddy are so very slow.

Once out of bed, I'm ready **to run**.

Outside my window, *it's dark*.

Where's the sun?

I scrub my hands without a hitch.

And brushing my teeth is really a cinch!

Time to go potty. **I can do this!**

Mommy is there to make sure *I don't miss.*

Onto the bed, where *I jump up and down.*
**Whee!** There's no time to waste as I flop around.
Mommy wrestles me into my clothes.
Daddy slides socks and shoes over my toes.

Wait! I want to tie *my own* shoes, **please!**

And *I'm certain* I can button **my coat** to my knees.

Before leaving for school, I have *some milk* to sip.
Mom grumbles about an **invisible hole** in my lip.

I grab my backpack, *ready for school!*
Daddy opens the door.
**Brrrr.** The air is cool.

Mommy gives me a kiss
and a *big bear hug*.

As I stroll toward the door,
I *trip over* the rug.

**I pick myself up**,
then I wave and smile.
Getting me into the *car seat*
takes a while.

Daddy walks me to my classroom.
I climb the steps **all by myself!**
I hang my coat on the hook and put my bag on the shelf.

The class is full of
*"Good mornings"* and *"Bye-byes."*
But this time, Daddy, **I won't cry.**

So many puzzles and toys,
I'm ready to play!
I hug Daddy *good-bye*,
I'm going to have a great day!